YUCK
Said The
Yak

By Alex English

Illustrated by Emma Levey

A hungry yak came to stay today.

"Hello, Yak!" said Alfie.

"Would you like some

toast and **jam?**"

"YUCK!"

said the yak.

"How about apples
picked fresh from
the tree?"

"YUCK!"

said the yak.

"That's not for me!"

"Would you like
eggs ...

or
peas...

or cheese...

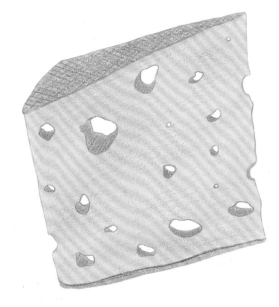

or strawberry jelly
with chocolate ice cream?"

But the yak said,

"YUCK!"

Alfie **poured**

and **stirred**

and **diced.**

He **baked**

and **squirted,**

scattered
and **sliced.**

Then Alfie threw down his plate and cup.

"You're a VERY rude yak and I GIVE UP!"

"But I'm a yak...

and yaks like grass!"

"Grass?"
said Alfie,
"How strange
to like
GRASS!"

"YUM!"

said the yak.

"Would you like a small bite?"

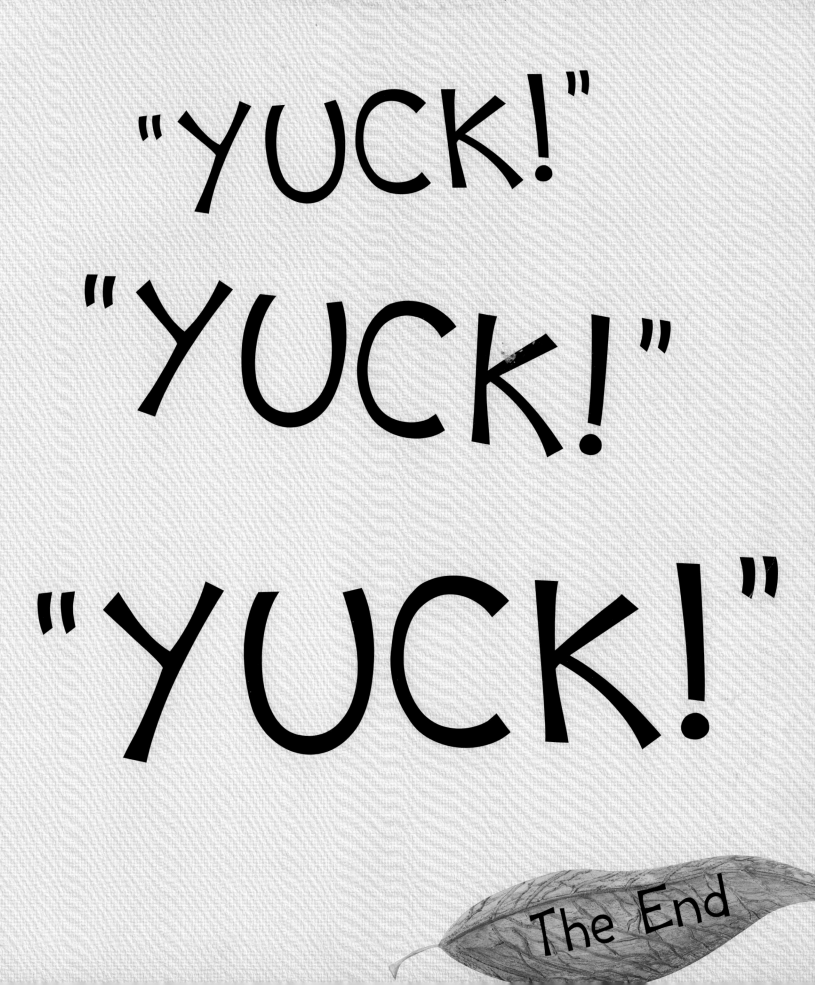

"Yuck!" said the Yak

An original concept by author Alex English

© Alex English

Illustrated by Emma Levey

First published September 2014

MAVERICK ARTS PUBLISHING LTD

Studio 3A, City Business Centre, 6 Brighton Road, Horsham, West Sussex, RH13 5BB

© Maverick Arts Publishing Limited September 2014 +44 (0)1403 256941

A CIP catalogue record for this book is available at the British Library.

Maverick

arts publishing

ISBN 978-1-84886-114-5